THE CITY OF
THE SINGING FLAME

THE CITY OF
THE SINGING FLAME

CLARK ASHTON SMITH

WILDSIDE PRESS

THE CITY OF THE SINGING FLAME

Originally published in *Wonder Stories,* July 1931.

Published by Wildside Press LLC.
www.wildsidebooks.com

FOREWORD

When Giles Angarth disappeared, nearly two years ago, we had been friends for a decade or more, and I knew him as well as anyone could purport to know him. Yet the thing was no less a mystery to me than to others at the time, and until now, it has remained a mystery.

Like the rest, I sometimes thought that he and Ebbonly had designed it all between them as a huge, insoluble hoax; that they were still alive, somewhere, and laughing at the world that was so sorely baffled by their disappearance. And, until I at last decided to visit Crater Ridge and find, if I could, the two boulders mentioned in Angarth's narrative, no one had uncovered any trace of the missing men or heard even the faintest rumor concerning them. The whole affair, it seemed then, was likely to remain a most singular and exasperating riddle.

Angarth, whose fame as a writer of fantastic fiction was already very considerable, had been spending that summer among the Sierras, and had been living alone until the artist, Felix Ebbonly, went to visit him. Ebbonly, whom I had never met, was well known for his imaginative paintings and drawings, and had illustrated more than one of Angarth's novels.

When neighboring campers became alarmed over the prolonged absence of the two men, and the cabin was searched for some possible clue, a package addressed to me was found lying on the table; and I received it in due course of time, after reading many newspaper speculations concerning the double vanishment. The package contained a small, leatherbound notebook, and Angarth had written on the flyleaf:

> Dear Hastane, You can publish this journal sometime, if you like. People will think it the last and wildest of all my fictions—unless they take it for one of your own. In either case, it will be just as well. Good-bye.
>   Faithfully,
>   GILES ANGARTH.

Feeling that it would certainly meet with the reception he anticipated, and being unsure, myself, whether the tale was truth or fabrication, I delayed publishing his journal. Now, from my own experience, I have become satisfied of its reality; and am finally printing it, together with an account of my personal adventures. Perhaps, the double publication, preceded as it is by Angarth's return to mundane surroundings, will help to ensure the acceptance of the whole story for more than mere fantasy.

Still, when I recall my own doubts, I wonder.... But let the reader decide for himself. And first, as to Giles Angarth's journal:

CHAPTER I

THE DIMENSION BEYOND

July 31st, 1938.—I have never acquired the diary-keeping habit—mainly, because of my uneventful, mode of existence, in which there has seldom been anything to chronicle. But the thing which happened this morning is so extravagantly strange, so remote from mundane laws and parallels, that I feel impelled to write it down to the best of my understanding and ability. Also, I shall keep account of the possible repetition and continuation of my experience. It will be perfectly safe to do this, for no one who ever reads the record will be likely to believe it....

I had gone for a walk on Crater Ridge, which lies a mile or less to the north of my cabin near Summit. Though differing markedly in its character from the usual landscapes round about, it is one of my favorite places. It is exceptionally bare and desolate, with little more in the way of vegetation than mountain sunflowers, wild currant bushes, and a few sturdy, wind-warped pines and supple tamaracks.

Geologists deny it a volcanic origin; yet its outcroppings of rough, nodular stone and enormous rubble-heaps have all the air of scoriac remains—at least, to my nonscientific eye. They look like the slag and refuse of Cyclopean furnaces, poured out in prehuman years, to cool and harden into shapes of limitless grotesquerie.

Among them are stones that suggest the fragments of primordial bas-reliefs, or small prehistoric idols and figurines; and others that seem to have been graven with lost letters of an indecipherable script. Unexpectedly, there is a little tarn lying on one end of the long, dry Ridge— a tarn that has never been fathomed. The hill is an odd interlude among the granite sheets and crags, and the fir-clothed ravines and valleys of this region.

It was a clear, windless morning, and I paused often to view the magnificent perspectives of varied scenery that were visible on every hand—the titan battlements of Castle Peak; the rude masses of Donner Peak, with its dividing pass of hemlocks; the remote, luminous blue of the Nevada Mountains, and the soft green of willows in the valley at my feet. It was an aloof, silent world, and I heard no sound other than the dry, crackling noise of cicadas among the currant-bushes.

I strolled on in a zigzag manner for some distance, and coming to one of the rubble-fields with which the Ridge is interstrewn, I began to search the ground closely, hoping to find a stone that was sufficiently quaint and grotesque in its form to be worth keeping as a curiosity: I had found several such in my previous wanderings. Suddenly, I came to a clear space amid the rubble, in which nothing grew—a space that was round as an artificial ring. In the center were two isolated boulders, queerly alike in shape, and lying about five feet apart.

I paused to examine them. Their substance, a dull, greenish-grey stone, seemed to be different from anything else in the neighborhood; and I conceived at once the weird, unwarrantable fancy that they might be the pedestals of vanished columns, worn away by incalculable years till there remained only these sunken ends. Certainly, the perfect roundness and uniformity of the boulders was peculiar, and though I possess a smattering of geology, I could not identify their smooth, soapy material.

My imagination was excited, and I began to indulge in some rather overheated fantasies. But the wildest of these was a homely commonplace in comparison with the thing that happened when I took a single step forward in the vacant space irnmediately between the two boulders. I shall try to describe it to the utmost of my ability; though human language is naturally wanting in words that are adequate for the delineation of events and sensations beyond the normal scope of human experience.

Nothing is more disconcerting than to miscalculate the degree of descent in taking a step. Imagine, then, what it was like to step forward on level, open ground, and find utter nothingness underfoot! I seemed to be going down into an empty gulf; and, at the same time, the landscape before me vanished in a swirl of broken images and everything went blind. There was a feeling of intense, hyperborean cold, and an indescribable sickness and vertigo possessed me, due, no doubt, to the profound disturbance of equilibrium. Either from the speed of my descent or for some other reason, I was, too, totally unable to draw breath.

My thoughts and feelings were unutterably confused, and half the time it seemed to me that I was falling upward rather than downward, or was sliding horizontally or at some oblique angle. At last, I had the sensation of turning a complete somersault; and then I found myself standing erect on solid ground once more, without the least shock or jar of impact. The darkness cleared away from my vision, but I was still dizzy, and the optical images I received were altogether meaningless for some moments.

When, finally, I recovered the power of cognisance and was able to view my surroundings with a measure of perception, I experienced a mental confusion equivalent to that of a man who might find himself cast without warning on the shore of some foreign planet. There was the same sense of utter loss and alienation which would assuredly be felt in such a case; the same vertiginous, overwhelming bewilderment, the same ghastly sense of separation from all the familiar environmental details that give color, form and definition to our lives and even determine our very personalities.

I was standing in the midst of a landscape which bore no degree or manner of resemblance to Crater Ridge. A long, gradual slope, covered with violet grass and studded at intervals with stones of monolithic size and shape, ran undulantly away beneath me to a broad plain with sinuous, open meadows and high, stately forests of an unknown vegetation whose predominant hues were purple and yellow. The plain seemed to end in a wall of impenetrable, golden-brownish mist, that rose with phantom pinnacles to dissolve on a sky of luminescent amber in which there was no sun.

In the foreground of this amazing scene, not more than two or three miles away, there loomed a city whose massive towers and mountainous ramparts of red stone were such as the Anakim of undiscovered worlds might build. Wall on beetling wall, spire on giant spire, it soared to confront the heavens, maintaining everywhere the severe and solemn lines of a rectilinear architecture. It seemed to overwhelm and crush down the beholder with its stern and craglike imminence.

As I viewed this city, I forgot my initial sense of bewildering loss and alienage, in an awe with which something of actual terror was mingled; and, at the same time, I felt an obscure but profound allurement, the cryptic emanation of some enslaving spell. But after I had gazed awhile, the cosmic strangeness and bafflement of my unthinkable position returned upon me, and I felt only a wild desire to escape from the maddeningly oppressive bizarrerie of this region and regain my own world. In an effort to fight down my agitation I tried to figure out, if possible, what had really happened.

I had read a number of transdimensional stories—in fact, I had written one or two myself; and I had often pondered the possibility of other worlds or material planes which may exist in the same space with ours, invisible and impalpable to human senses. Of course, I realized at once that I had fallen into some such dimension. Doubtless, when I took that step forward between the boulders, I had been precipitated into some sort of flaw or fissure in space, to emerge at the bottom in this alien sphere—in a totally different kind of space.

It sounded simple enough, in a way, but not simple enough to make the modus operandi anything but a brain-racking mystery, and in a further effort to collect myself, I studied my immediate surroundings with a close attention. This time, I was impressed by the arrangement of the monolithic stones I have spoken of, many of which were disposed at fairly regular intervals in two parallel lines running down the hill, as if to mark the course of some ancient road obliterated by the purple grass.

Turning to follow its ascent, I saw right behind me two columns, standing at precisely the same distance apart as the two odd boulders on Crater Ridge, and formed of the same soapy, greenish-gray stone. The pillars were perhaps nine feet high, and had been taller at one time, since the tops were splintered and broken away. Not far above them, the mounting slope vanished from view in a great bank of the same golden-brown mist that enveloped the remoter plain. But there were no more monoliths, and it seemed as if the road had ended with those pillars.

Inevitably, I began to speculate as to the relationship between the columns in this new dimension and the boulders in my own world. Surely, the resemblance could not be a matter of mere chance. If I stepped between the columns, could I return to the human sphere by a reversal of my precipitation therefrom? And if so, by what inconceivable beings from foreign time and space had the columns and boulders been established as the portals of a gateway between the two worlds? Who could have used the gateway, and for what purpose?

My brain reeled before the infinite vistas of surmise that were opened by such questions. However, what concerned me most was the problem of getting back to Crater Ridge. The weirdness of it all, the monstrous walls of the nearby town, the unnatural hues and forms of the outlandish scenery, were too much for human nerves, and I felt that I should go mad if forced to remain long in such a milieu. Also, there was no telling what hostile powers or entities I might encounter if I stayed.

The slope and plain were devoid of animate life, as far as I could see; but the great city was presumptive proof of its existence. Unlike the heroes in my own tales, who were wont to visit the Fifth Dimension or the worlds of Algol with perfect sang froid, I did not feel in the least adventurous, and I shrank back with man's instinctive recoil before the unknown. With one fearful glance at the looming city and the wide plain with its lofty gorgeous vegetation, I turned and stepped back between the columns.

There was the same instantaneous plunge into blind and freezing gulfs, the same indeterminate falling and twisting, which had marked my descent into this new dimension. At the end I found myself standing, very dizzy and shaken, on the sane spot from which I had taken my forward step between the greenish-gray boulders. Crater Ridge was swirling and reeling about me as if in the throes of earthquake, and I had to sit down for a minute or two before I could recover my equilibrium.

I came back to the cabin like a man in a dream. The experience seemed, and still seems, incredible and unreal; and yet it has overshadowed everything else, and has colored and dominated all my thoughts. Perhaps, by writing it down, I can shake it off a little. It has unsettled me more than any previous experience in my whole life, and the world about me seems hardly less improbable and nightmarish than the one which I have penetrated in a fashion so fortuitous.

August 2nd.—I have done a lot of thinking in the past few days, and the more I ponder and puzzle, the more mysterious it all becomes. Granting the flaw in space, which must be an absolute vacuum, impervious to air, ether, light and matter, how was it possible for me to fall into it? And having fallen in, how could I fall out—particularly into a sphere that has no certifiable relationship with ours?

But, after all, one process would be as easy as the other, in theory. The main objection is: how could one move in a vacuum, either up or down, or backward or forward? The whole thing would baffle the comprehension of an Einstein, and I cannot feel that I have even approached the true solution.

Also, I have been fighting the temptation to go back, if only to convince myself that the thing really occurred.

But, after all, why shouldn't I go back? An opportunity has been vouchsafed to me such as no man may even have been given before, and the wonders I shall see, the secrets I shall learn, are beyond imagining. My nervous trepidation is inexcusably childish under the circumstances....

CHAPTER II

THE TITAN CITY

August 3rd.—I went back this morning, armed with a revolver. Somehow, without thinking that it might make a difference, I did not step in the very middle of the space between the boulders. Undoubtedly, as a result of this, my descent was more prolonged and impetuous than before, and seemed to consist mainly of a series of spiral somersaults. It must have taken me several minutes to recover from the ensuing vertigo, and when I came to, I was lying on the violet grass.

This time, I went boldly down the slope, and keeping as much as I could in the shelter of the bizarre purple and yellow vegetation, I stole toward the looming city. All was very still; there was no breath of wind in those exotic trees, which appeared to imitate, in their lofty, upright boles and horizontal foliage, the severe architectural lines of the Cyclopean buildings.

I had not gone far when I came to a road in the forest— a road paved with stupendous blocks of stone at least twenty feet square. It ran toward the city. I thought for a while that it was wholly deserted, perhaps disused; and I even dared to walk upon it, till I heard a noise behind me and, turning, saw the approach of several singular entities. Terrified, I sprang back and hid myself in a thicket, from which I watched the passing of those creatures, wondering fearfully if they had seen me. Apparently, my fears were groundless, for they did not even glance at my hiding place.

It is hard for me to describe or even visualize them now, for they were totally unlike anything that we are accustomed to think of as human or animal. They must have been ten feet tall, and they were moving along with colossal strides that took them from sight in a few instants, beyond a turn of the road. Their bodies were bright and shining, as if encased in some sort of armor, and their heads were equipped with high, curving appendages of opalescent hues which nodded above them like fantastic plumes, but may have been antennae or other sense-organs of a novel type. Trembling with excitement and wonder, I continued my progress through the richly colored undergrowth. As I went on, I perceived for the first time that there were no shadows anywhere. The light came from all portions of the sunless, amber heaven, pervading everything with a soft, uniform luminosity. All was motionless and silent, as before; and there was no evidence of bird, insect or animal life in all this preternatural landscape.

But, when I had advanced to within a mile of the city— as well as I could judge the distance in a realm where the very proportions of objects were unfamiliar—I became aware of something which at first was recognizable as a vibration rather than a sound. There was a queer thrilling in my nerves; the disquieting sense of some unknown force or emanation flowing through my body. This was perceptible for some time before I heard the music, but having heard it, my auditory nerves identified it at once with the vibration.

It was faint and far-off, and seemed to emanate from the very heart of the Titan city. The melody was piercingly sweet, and resembled at times the singing of some voluptuous feminine voice. However, no human voice could have possessed that unearthly pitch, the shrill, perpetually sustained notes that somehow suggested the light of remote worlds and stars translated into sound.

Ordinarily, I am not very sensitive to music; I have even been reproached for not reacting more strongly to it. But I had not gone much farther when I realized the peculiar mental and emotional spell which the far-off sound was beginning to exert upon me. There was a sirenlike allurement which drew me on, forgetful of the strangeness and potential perils of my situation; and I felt a slow, druglike intoxication of brain and senses.

In some insidious manner, I know not how nor why, the music conveyed the ideas of vast but attainable space and altitude, of superhuman freedom and exultation; and it seemed to promise all the impossible splendors of which my imagination has vaguely dreamt....

The forest continued almost to the city walls. Peering from behind the final boscage, I saw their overwhelming battlements in the sky above me, and noted the flawless jointure of their prodigious blocks. I was near the great road, which entered an open gate large enough to admit the passage of behemoths. There were no guards in sight, and several more of the tall, gleaming entities came striding along and went in as I watched.

From where I stood, I was unable to see inside the gate, for the wall was stupendously thick. The music poured from that mysterious entrance in an ever-strengthening flood, and sought to draw me on with its weird seduction, eager for unimaginable things. It was hard to resist; hard to rally my willpower and turn back. I tried to concentrate on the thought of danger—but the thought was tenuously unreal.

At last, I tore myself away and retraced my footsteps, very slowly and lingeringly, till I was beyond reach of the music. Even then, the spell persisted, like the effects of a drug; and all the way home I was tempted to return and follow those shining giants into the city.

August 5th.—I have visited the new dimension once more. I thought I could resist that summoning music, and I even took some cotton-wadding with which to stuff my ears if it should affect me too strongly. I began to hear the supernal melody at the same distance as before, and was drawn onward in the same manner. But, this time, I entered the open gate!

I wonder if I can describe that city? I felt like a crawling ant upon its mammoth pavements, amid the measureless Babel of its buildings, of its streets and arcades. Everywhere there were columns, obelisks and the perpendicular pylons of fanelike structures that would have dwarfed those of Thebes and Heliopolis. And the people of the city! How is one to depict them, or give them a name!

I think that the gleaming entities I first saw are not the true inhabitants, but are only visitors, perhaps from some other world or dimension, like myself. The real people are giants, too; but they move slowly, with solemn, hieratic paces. Their bodies are nude and swart, and their limbs are those of caryatides—massive enough, it would seem, to uphold the roofs and lintels of their own buildings. I fear to describe them minutely, for human words would give the idea of something monstrous and uncouth, and these beings are not monstrous, but they have merely developed in obedience to the laws of another evolution than ours; the environmental forces and conditions of a different world.

Somehow, I was not afraid when I saw then—perhaps the music had dragged me till I was beyond fear. There was a group of them just inside the gate, and they seemed to pay me no attention whatever as I passed them. The opaque, jetlike orbs of their huge eyes were impassive as the carven eyes of androsphinxes, and they uttered no sound from their heavy, straight, expressionless lips. Perhaps they lack the sense of hearing, for their strange, semi-rectangular heads were devoid of anything in the nature of external ears.

I followed the music, which was still remote and seemed to increase little in loudness. I was soon overtaken by several of those beings whom I had previously seen on the road outside the walls; and they passed me quickly and disappeared in the labyrinth of buildings. After them there came other beings of a less gigantic kind, and without the bright shards or armor worn by the first-comers. Then, overhead, two creatures with long, translucent, blood-colored wings, intricately veined and ribbed, came flying side by side and vanished behind the others. Their faces, featured with organs of unsurmisable use, were ant those of animals, and I felt sure that they were beings of a high order of development.

I saw hundreds of those slow-moving, somber entities whom I have identified as the true inhabitants, but none of them appeared to notice me. Doubtless they were accustomed to seeing far weirder and more unusual kinds of life than humanity. As I went on, I was overtaken by dozens of improbable-looking creatures, all going in the same direction as myself, as if drawn by the same siren melody.

Deeper and deeper I went into the wilderness of colossal architecture, led by that remote, ethereal, opiate music. I soon noticed a sort of gradual ebb and flow in the sound, occupying an interval of ten minutes or more; but, by imperceptible degrees, it grew sweeter and nearer. I wondered how it could penetrate that manifold maze of builded stone and be heard outside the walls....

I must have walked for miles, in the ceaseless gloom of those rectangular structures that hung above me, tier on tier, at an awful height in the amber zenith. Then, at length, I came to the core and secret of it all. Preceded and followed by a number of those chimerical entities, I emerged on a great square, in whose center was a temple-like building more immense than the others. The music poured, imperiously shrill and loud, from its many-columned entrance.

I felt the thrill of one who approaches the sanctum of some hierarchal mystery, when I entered the halls of that building. People who must have come from many different worlds or dimensions went with me, and before me, along the titanic colonnades, whose pillars were graven with indecipherable runes and enigmatic bas-reliefs. The dark, colossal inhabitants of the town were standing or roaming about, intent, like all the others, on their own affairs. None of these beings spoke, either to me or to one another, and though several eyed me casually, my presence was evidently taken for granted.

There are no words to convey the incomprehensible wonder of it all. And the music? I have utterly failed to describe that, also. It was as if some marvelous elixir had been turned into sound-waves—an elixir conferring the gift of superhuman life, and the high, magnificent dreams which are dreamt by the Immortals. It mounted in my brain like a supernal drunkenness, as I approached the hidden source. I do not know what obscure warning prompted me, now, to stuff my ears with cotton before I went any farther. Though I could still hear it, still feel its peculiar, penetrant vibration, the sound became muted when I had done this, and its influence was less powerful henceforth. There is little doubt that I owe my life to this simple and homely precaution.

The endless rows of columns grew dim for a while as the interior of a long, basaltic cavern; and then, some distance ahead, I perceived the glimmering of a soft light on the floor and pillars. The light soon became an over-flooding radiance, as if gigantic lamps were being lit in the temple's heart; and the vibrations of the hidden music pulsed more strongly in my nerves.

The hall ended in a chamber of immense, indefinite scope, whose walls and roof were doubtful with unre-moving shadows. In the center, amid the pavement of mammoth blocks, there was a circular pit, above which seemed to float a fountain of flame that soared in one perpetual, slowly lengthening jet. This flame was the sole illumination, and also, was the source of the wild, unearthly music. Even with my purposely deafened ears, I was wooed by the shrill and starry sweetness of its sing-ing; and I felt the voluptuous lure and the high, vertigi-nous exaltation.

I knew immediately that the place was a shrine, and that the transdimensional beings who accompanied me were visiting pilgrims. There were scores of them—per-haps hundreds; but all were dwarfed in the cosmic im-mensity of that chamber. They were gathered before the flame in various attitudes of worship; they bowed their exotic heads, or made mysterious gestures or adoration with unhuman hands and members. And the voices of several, deep as booming drums, or sharp as the stridula-tion of giant insects, were audible amid the singing of the fountain.

Spellbound, I went forward and joined them. En-thralled by the music and by the vision of the soaring flame, I paid as little heed to my outlandish companions as they to me. The fountain rose and rose, until its light flickered on the limbs and features of throned, colossal, statues behind it—of heroes, gods or demons from the earlier cycles of alien time, staring in stone from a dusk of illimitable mystery.

The fire was green and dazzling, pure as the central flame of a star; it blinded me, and when I turned my eyes away, the air was filled with webs of intricate colour, with swiftly changing arabesques whose numberless, unwonted hues and patterns were such as no mundane eye had ever beheld. And I felt a stimulating warmth that filled my very marrow with intenser life.…

CHAPTER III

THE LURE OF THE FLAME

The music mounted with the flame; and I understood, now, its recurrent ebb and flow. As I looked and listened, a mad thought was born in my mind—the thought of how marvelous and ecstatical it would be to run forward and leap headlong into the singing fire. The music seemed to tell me that I should find in that moment of flaring dissolution all the delight and triumph, all the splendor and exaltation it had promised from afar. It besought me; it pleaded with tones of supernal melody, and despite the wadding in my ears, the seduction was well-nigh irresistible.

However, it had not robbed me of all sanity. With a sudden start of terror, like one who has been tempted to fling himself from a high precipice, I drew back. Then I saw that the same dreadful impulse was shared by some of my companions. The two entities with scarlet wings, whom I have previously mentioned, were standing a little apart from the rest of us. Now, with a great fluttering, they rose and flew toward the flame like moths toward a candle. For a brief moment the light shone redly through their half transparent wings, ere they disappeared in the leaping incandescence, which flared briefly and then burned as before.

Then, in rapid succession, a number of other beings, who represented the most divergent trends of biology, sprang forward and immolated themselves in the flame. There were creatures with translucent bodies, and some that shone with all the hues of the opal; there were winged colossi, and Titans who strode as with seven-league boots; and there was one being with useless, abortive wings, who crawled rather than ran, to seek the same glorious doom as the rest. But among them there were none of the city's people: these merely stood and looked on, impassive and statuelike as ever.

I saw that the fountain had now reached its greatest height, and was beginning to decline. It sank steadily, but slowly, to half its former elevation. During this interval, there were no more acts of self-sacrifice, and several of the beings beside me turned abruptly and went away, as if they had overcome the lethal spell.

One of the tall, armored entities, as he left, addressed me in words that were like clarion-notes, with unmistakable accents of warning. By a mighty effort of will, in a turmoil of conflicting emotions, I followed him. At every step, the madness and delirium of the music warred with my instincts of self-preservation. More than once, I started to go back. My homeward journey was blurred and doubtful as the wanderings of a man in opium-trance; and the music sang behind me, and told me of the rapture I had missed, of, the flaming dissolution whose brief instant was better than aeons of mortal life....

August 9th.—I have tried to go on with a new story, but have made no progress. Anything that I can imagine, or frame in language, seems flat and puerile beside the world of unsearchable mystery to which I have found admission. The temptation to return is more cogent than ever; the call of that remembered music is sweeter than the voice of a loved woman. And always I am tormented by the problem of it all, and tantalized by the little which I have perceived and understood.

What forces are these whose existence and working I have merely apprehended? Who are the inhabitants of the city? And who are the beings that visit the enshrined flame? What rumor or legend has drawn them from outland realms and ulterior planets to that place of inenarrable danger and destruction? And what is the fountain itself, what the secret of its lure and its deadly singing? These problems admit of infinite surmise, but no conceivable solution.

I am planning to go back once more ... but not alone. Someone must go with me, this time, as a witness to the wonder and the peril. It is all too strange for credence: I must have human corroboration of what I have seen and felt and conjectured. Also, another might understand where I have failed to do more than apprehend.

Who shall I take? It will be necessary to invite someone here from the outer world—someone of high intellectual and aesthetic capacity. Shall I ask Philip Hastane, my fellow fiction-writer? He would be too busy, I fear. But there is the Californian artist, Felix Ebbonly, who has illustrated some of my fantastic novels....

Ebbonly would be the man to see and appreciate the new dimension, if he can come. With his bent for the bizarre and unearthly, the spectacle of that plain and city, the Babelian buildings and arcades, and the Temple of the Flame, will simply enthrall him. I shall write immediately to his San Francisco address.

August 12th.—Ebbonly is here: the mysterious hints in my letter, regarding some novel pictorial subjects along his own line, were too provocative for him to resist. Now, I have explained fully and given him a detailed account of my adventures. I can see that he is a little incredulous, for which I hardly blame him. But he will not remain incredulous for long, for tomorrow we shall visit together the City of the Singing Flame.

August 13th.—I must concentrate my disordered faculties, must choose my words and write with exceeding care. This will be the last entry in my journal, and the last writing I shall ever do. When I have finished, I shall wrap the journal up and address it to Philip Hastane, who can make such disposition of it as he sees fit.

I took Ebbonly into the other dimension today. He was impressed, even as I had been, by the two isolated boulders on Crater Ridge.

"They look like the guttered ends of columns established by prehuman gods," he remarked. "I begin to believe you now."

I told him to go first, and indicated the place where he should step. He obeyed without hesitation, and I had the singular experience of seeing a man melt into utter, instantaneous nothingness. One moment he was there—the next, there was only bare ground, and the far-off tamaracks whose view his body had obstructed. I followed, and found him standing, in speechless awe, on the violet grass.

"This," he said at last, "is the sort of thing whose existence I have hitherto merely suspected, and have never been able to hint at in my most imaginative drawings."

We spoke little as we followed the range of monolithic boulders toward the plain. Far in the distance, beyond those high and stately trees, with their sumptuous foliage, the golden-brown vapors had parted, showing vistas of an immense horizon; and past the horizon were range on range of gleaming orbs and fiery, flying motes in the depth of that amber heaven. It was as if the veil of another universe than ours had been drawn back.

We crossed the plain, and came at length within earshot of the siren music. I warned Ebbonly to stuff his ears with cotton-wadding, but he refused.

"I don't want to deaden any new sensation I may experience," he observed.

We entered the city. My companion was in a veritable rhapsody of artistic delight when he beheld the enormous buildings and the people. I could see, too, that the music had taken hold upon him: his look soon became fixed and dreamy as that of an opium-eater.

At first, he made many comments on the architecture and the various beings who passed us, and called my attention to details which I had not perceived before. However, as we drew nearer the Temple of the Flame, his observational interest seemed to flag, and was replaced by more and more of an ecstatic inward absorption. His remarks became fewer and briefer, and he did not even seem to hear my questions. It was evident that the sound had wholly bemused and bewitched him.

Even as on my former visit, there were many pilgrims going toward the shrine—and few that were coming away from it. Most of them belonged to evolutionary types that I had seen before. Among those that were new to me, I recall one gorgeous creature with golden and cerulean wings like those of a giant lepidoptera, and scintillating, jewellike eyes that must have been designed to mirror the glories of some Edenic world.

I felt, too, as before, the captious thraldom and bewitchment, the insidious, gradual perversion of thought and instinct, as if the music were working in my brain like a subtle alkaloid. Since I had taken my usual precaution, my subjection to the influence was less complete than that of Ebbonly; but, nevertheless, it was enough to make me forget a number of things—among them, the initial concern which I had felt when my companion refused to employ the same mode of protection as myself. I no longer thought of his danger, or my own, except as something very distant and immaterial.

The streets were like the prolonged and bewildering labyrinth of a nightmare. But the music led us forthrightly, and always there were other pilgrims. Like men in the grip of some powerful current, we were drawn to our destination. As we passed along the hall of gigantic columns and neared the abode of the fiery fountain, a sense of our peril quickened momentarily in my brain, and I sought to warn Ebbonly once more. But all my protests and remonstrances were futile: he was deaf as a machine, and wholly impervious to anything but the lethal music. His expression and movements were those of a somnambulist. Even when I seized and shook him with such violence as I could muster, he remained oblivious of my presence.

The throng of worshippers was larger than upon my first visit. The jet of pure, incandescent flame was mounting steadily as we entered, and it sang with the pure ardor and ecstasy of a star alone in space. Again, with ineffable tones, it told me the rapture of a mothlike death in its lofty soaring, the exultation and triumph of a momentary union with its elemental essence.

The flame rose to its apex; and even for me, the mesmeric lure was well-nigh irresistible. Many of our companions succumbed, and the first to immolate himself was the giant lepidopterous being. Four others, of diverse evolutional types, followed in appallingly swift succession.

In my own partial subjection to the music, my own effort to resist that deadly enslavement, I had almost forgotten the very presence of Ebbonly. It was too late for me to even think of stopping him, when he ran forward in a series of leaps that were both solemn and frenzied, like the beginnings of some sacerdotal dance, and hurled himself headlong into the flame. The fire enveloped him; it flared up for an instant with a more dazzling greenness, and that was all.

Slowly, as if from benumbed brain centers, a horror crept upon my conscious mind, and helped to annul the perilous mesmerism. I turned, while many others were following Ebbonly's example, and fled from the shrine and from the city. But somehow the horror diminished as I went; more and more, I found myself envying my companion's fate, and wondering as to the sensations he had felt in that moment of fiery dissolution....

Now, as I write this, I am wondering why I came back again to the human world. Words are futile to express what I have beheld and experienced, and the change that has come upon me, beneath the play of incalculable forces in a world of which no other mortal is even cognisant. Literature is nothing more than a shadow. Life, with its drawn-out length of monotonous, reiterative days, is unreal and without meaning, now, in comparison with the splendid death which I might have had—the glorious doom which is still in store.

I have no longer any will to fight the ever-insistent music which I hear in memory. And there seems to be no reason at all why I should fight it.... Tomorrow, I shall return to the city.

CHAPTER IV

THE THIRD VENTURER

Even when I, Philip Hastane, had read through the journal of my friend, Giles Angarth, so many times that I had almost learned it by heart, I was still doubtful as to whether the incidents related therein were fiction or verity. The transdimensional adventures of Angarth and Ebbonly; the City of the Flame, with its strange residents and pilgrims; the immolation of Ebbonly, and the hinted return of the narrator himself for a like purpose, in the last entry of the diary, were very much the sort of thing that Angarth might have imagined in one of the fantastic novels for which he had become so justly famous. Add to this the seemingly impossible and incredible nature of the whole tale, and my hesitancy in accepting it as veridical will easily be understood.

However, on the other hand, there was the unsolved and recalcitrant enigma offered by the disappearance of the two men. Both were well known, one as a writer, the other as an artist; both were in flourishing circumstances, with no serious cares or troubles; and their vanishment, all things considered, was difficult to explain on the ground of any motive less unusual or extraordinary than the one assigned in the journal. At first, as I have mentioned in my foreword to the diary, I thought the whole affair might well have been devised as a somewhat elaborate practical joke; but this theory became less and less tenable as weeks and months went by, and linked themselves slowly into a year, without the reappearance of the presumptive jokers.

Now, at last, I can testify to the truth of all that Angarth wrote—and more. For I, too, have been in Ydmos, the City of Singing Flame, and have known also the supernal glories and raptures of the Inner Dimension. And of these I must tell, however falteringly and inadequately, with mere human words, before the vision fades. For these are things which neither I, nor any other, shall behold or experience again.

Ydmos itself is now a riven ruin; the Temple of the Flame has been blasted to its foundations in the basic rock, and the fountain of singing fire has been stricken at its source. The Inner Dimension has perished like a broken bubble, in the great war that was made upon Ydmos by the rulers of the Outer Lands....

After having finally laid down Angarth's journal, I was unable to forget the peculiar and tantalizing problems it raised. The vague, but infinitely suggestive vistas opened by the tale were such as to haunt my imagination recurrently with a hint of half-revealed mysteries. I was troubled by the possibility of some great and mystic meaning behind it all; some cosmic actuality of which the narrator had perceived merely the external veils and fringes. As time went on, I found myself pondering it perpetually, and becoming more and more possessed by an overwhelming wonder, and a sense of something which no mere action-weaver would have been likely to invent.

In the early summer of 1939, after finishing a new novel, I felt able for the first time to take the necessary leisure for the execution of a project that had often occurred to me. Putting all my affairs in order, and knitting all the loose ends of my literary labours and correspondence, in case I should not return, I left my home in Auburn, ostensibly for a week's vacation. Actually, I went to Summit, with the idea of investigating closely the milieu in which Angarth and Ebbonly had disappeared from human ken.

With strange emotions, I visited the forsaken cabin south of Crater Ridge, that had been occupied by Angarth, and saw the rough table of pine boards upon which my friend had written his journal, and then left the sealed package containing it to be forwarded to me after his departure.

There was a weird and brooding loneliness about the place, as if the nonhuman infinitudes had already claimed it for their own. The unlocked door had sagged inward from the pressure of high-piled winter snows, and fir needles had sifted across the sill to strew the unswept floor. Somehow, I know not why, the bizarre narrative became more real and more credible to me, while I stood there, as if an occult intimation of all that had happened to its author still lingered around the cabin.

This mysterious intimation grew stronger when I came to visit Crater Ridge itself, and to search amid its miles of pseudo-volcanic rubble for the two boulders so explicitly described by Angarth as having a likeness to the pedestals of ruined columns. Following the northward path which he must have taken from his cabin, and trying to retrace his wanderings of the long, barren hill, I combed it thoroughly from end to end and from side to side, since he had not specified the location of the boulders. And after two mornings spent in this manner, without result, I was almost ready to abandon the quest and dismiss the queer, soapy, greenish-gray column-ends as one of Angarth's most provocative and deceptive fictions.

It must have been the formless, haunting intuition to which I have referred, that made me renew the search on the third morning. This time, after crossing and recrossing the hilltop for an hour or more, and weaving tortuously among the cicada-haunted wild-currant bushes and sunflowers on the dusty slopes, I came at last to an open, circular, rock-surrounded space that was totally unfamiliar. I had somehow missed it in all my previous roamings. It was the place of which Angarth had told; and I saw, with an inexpressible thrill, the two rounded, worn-looking boulders that were situated in the center of the ring.

I believe that I trembled a little with excitement, as I went forward to inspect the curious stones. Bending over, but not daring to enter the bare, pebbly space between them, I touched one of them with my hand, and received a sensation of preternatural smoothness, together with a coolness that was inexplicable, considering that the boulders and the soil about them must have lain unshaded from the sultry August sun for many hours.

From that moment, I became fully persuaded that Angarth's account was no mere fable. Just why I should have felt so certain of this, I am powerless to say. But it seemed to me that I stood on the threshold of an ultramundane mystery, on the brink of uncharted gulfs. I looked about at the familiar Sierran valleys and mountains, wondering that they still preserved their wonted outlines, and were still unchanged by the contiguity of alien worlds, still untouched by the luminous glories of arcanic dimensions.

Convinced that I had indeed found the gateway between the worlds, I was prompted to strange reflections. What, and where, was this other sphere to which my friend had attained entrance? Was it near at hand, like a secret room in the structure of space? Or was it, in reality, millions or trillions of lightyears away, by the reckoning of astronomic distance, in a planet of some ulterior galaxy?

After all, we know little or nothing of the actual nature of space; and, perhaps, in some way that we cannot imagine, the infinite is doubled upon itself in places, with dimensional folds and tucks, and shortcuts whereby the distance to Algenib or Aldebaran is but a step. Perhaps, also, there is more than one infinity. The spatial "flaw" into which Angarth had fallen might well be a sort of super-dimension, abridging the cosmic intervals and connecting universe with universe.

However, because of this very certitude that I had found the inter-spheric portals, and could follow Angarth and Ebbonly if I so desired, I hesitated before trying the experiment. I was mindful of the mystic danger and irrefragable lure that had overcome the others. I was consumed by imaginative curiosity, by an avid, well-nigh feverish longing to behold the wonders of this exotic realm; but I did not purpose to become a victim to the opiate power and fascination of the Singing Flame.

I stood for a long time, eyeing the odd boulders and the barren, pebble-littered spot that gave admission to the unknown. At length, I went away, deciding to defer my venture till the following morning. Visualizing the weird doom to which the others had gone so voluntarily, and even gladly, I must confess that I was afraid. On the other hand, I was drawn by the fateful allurement that leads an explorer into far places ... and, perhaps, by something more than this.

I slept badly that night, with nerves and brain excited by formless, glowing premonitions, by intimations of half conceived perils, and splendors and vastnesses. Early the next morning, while the sun was still hanging above the Nevada Mountains, I returned to Crater Ridge.

I carried a strong hunting-knife and a Colt revolver, and wore a filled cartridge-belt, with a knapsack containing sandwiches and a thermos bottle of coffee.

Before starting, I had stuffed my ears tightly with cotton soaked in a new anaesthetic fluid, mild but efficacious, which would serve to deafen me completely for many hours. In this way, I felt that I should be immune to the demoralizing music of the fiery fountain. I peered about at the rugged landscape with its far-flung vistas, wondering if I should ever see it again. Then, resolutely, but with the eerie thrilling and sinking of one who throws himself from a high cliff into some bottomless chasm, I stepped forward into the space between the grayish-green boulders.

My sensations, generally speaking, were similar to those described by Angarth in his diary. Blackness and illimitable emptiness seemed to wrap me round in a dizzy swirl as of rushing wind or milling water, and I went down and down in a spiral descent whose duration I have never been able to estimate. Intolerably stifled, and without even the power to gasp for breath, in the chill, airless vacuum that froze my very muscles and marrow, I felt that I should lose consciousness in another moment and descend into the greater gulf of death or oblivion.

Something seemed to arrest my fall, and I became aware that I was standing still, though I was troubled for some time by a queer doubt as to whether my position was vertical, horizontal or upside-down in relation to the solid substance that my feet had encountered. Then, the blackness lifted slowly like a dissolving cloud, and I saw the slope of violet grass, the rows of irregular monoliths running downward from where I stood, and the gray-green columns near at hand. Beyond was the titan, perpendicular city of red stone that was dominant above the high and multi-coloured vegetation of the plain.

It was all very much as Angarth had depicted it; but somehow, even then, I became aware of differences that were not immediately or clearly definable, of scenic details and atmospheric elements for which his account had not prepared me. And, at the moment I was too thoroughly disequilibrated and overpowered by the vision of it all to even speculate concerning the character of these differences.

As I gazed at the city, with its crowding tiers of battlements and its multitude of overlooming spires I felt the invisible threads of a secret attraction, was seized by an imperative longing to know the mysteries hidden behind the massive walls and the myriad buildings. Then, a moment later, my gaze was drawn to the remote, opposite horizon of the plain, as if by some conflicting impulse whose nature and origin were undiscoverable.

It must have been because I had formed so clear and definite a picture of the scene from my friend's narrative, that I was surprised, and even a little disturbed as if by something wrong or irrelevant, when I saw in the far distance the shining towers of what seemed to be another city—a city of which Angarth had not written. The towers rose in serried lines, reaching for many miles in a curious arclike formation, and were sharply defined against a blackish mass of cloud that had reared behind them and was spreading out on the luminous, amber sky in sullen webs and sinister, crawling filaments.

Subtle disquietude and repulsion seemed to emanate from the far-off, glittering spires, even as attraction emanated from those of the nearer city. I saw them quiver and pulse with an evil light, like living and moving things, through what I assumed to be some refractive trick of the atmosphere. Then, for an instant, the black cloud behind them glowed with dull, angry crimson throughout its whole mass, and even its questing webs and tendrils were turned into lurid threads of fire.

The crimson faded, leaving the cloud inert and lumpish as before; but from many of the vanward towers, lines of red and violet flame had leaped, like out-thrust lances, at the bosom of the plain beneath them. They were held thus for at least a minute, moving slowly across a wide area, before they vanished. In the spaces between the towers, I now perceived a multitude of gleaming, restless particles, like armies of militant atoms, and wondered if perchance they were living things. If the idea had not appeared so fantastical, I could have sworn, even then, that the far city had already changed its position and was advancing toward the other on the plain.

CHAPTER V

THE STRIDING DOOM

Apart from the fulguration of the cloud, the flames that had sprung from the towers, and the quiverings which I deemed a refractive phenomenon, the whole landscape before and about me was unnaturally still. On the strange amber air, the Tyrian-tinted grasses, and the proud, opulent foliage of the unknown trees, where lay the dead calm that precedes the stupendous turmoil of typhonic storm or seismic cataclysm. The brooding sky was permeated with intuitions of cosmic menace, and weighed down by a dim, elemental despair.

Alarmed by this ominous atmosphere, I looked behind me at the two pillars which, according to Angarth, were the gateway of return to the human world. For an instant, I was tempted to go back. Then, I turned once more to the nearby city, and the feelings I have mentioned were lost in an oversurging awesomeness and wonder. I felt the thrill of a deep, supernal exaltation before the magnitude of the mighty buildings; a compelling sorcery was laid upon me by the very lines of their construction, by the harmonies of a solemn architectural music. I forgot my impulse to return to Crater Ridge, and started down the slope toward the city.

Soon the boughs of the purple and yellow forest arched above me like the altitudes of Titan-builded aisles, with leaves that fretted the rich heaven in gorgeous arabesques.

Beyond them, ever and anon, I caught glimpses of the piled ramparts of my destination; but looking back in the direction of that other city on the horizon, I found that its fulgurating towers were now lost to view.

I saw, however, that the masses of the great somber cloud were rising steadily on the sky, and once again they flared to a swart, malignant red, as if with some unearthly form of sheet-lightning; and though I could hear nothing with my deadened ears, the ground beneath me trembled with long vibrations as of thunder. There was a queer quality in the vibrations, that seemed to tear my nerves and set my teeth on edge with its throbbing, lancinating discord, painful as broken glass or the torment of a tightened rack.

Like Angarth before me, I came to the paved Cyclopean highway. Following it, in the stillness after the unheard peals of thunder, I felt another and subtler vibration, which I knew to be that of the Singing Flame in the temple at the city's core. It seemed to soothe and exalt and bear me on, to erase with soft caresses the ache that still lingered in my nerves from the torturing pulsations of the thunder.

I met no one on the road, and was not passed by any of the trans-dimensional pilgrims such as had overtaken Angarth; and when the accumulated ramparts loomed above the highest trees I came forth from the wood in their very shadow, I saw that the great gate of the city was closed, leaving no crevice through which a pygmy like myself might obtain entrance.

Feeling a profound and peculiar discomfiture, such as one would experience in a dream that had gone wrong, I stared at the grim, unrelenting blackness of the gate, which seemed to be wrought from one enormous sheet of somber and lustreless metal. Then, I peered upward at the sheerness of the wall, which rose above me like an alpine cliff, and saw that the battlements were seemingly deserted. Was the city forsaken by its people, by the guardians of the Flame? Was it no longer open to the pilgrims who came from outlying lands to worship the Flame and immolate themselves?

With a curious reluctance, after lingering there for many minutes in a sort of stupor, I turned away to retrace my steps. In the interim of my journey, the black cloud had drawn immeasurably nearer, and was now blotting out half the heaven with two portentous, winglike formations. It was a sinister and terrible sight; and it lightened again with that ominous, wrathful flaming, with a detonation that beat upon my deaf ears like waves of disintegrative force, and seemed to lacerate the inmost fibers of my body.

I hesitated, fearing that the storm would burst upon me before I could reach the inter-dimensional portals, for I saw that I should be exposed to an elemental disturbance of unfamiliar character and supreme violence. Then, in mid air before the imminent, ever-rising cloud, I perceived two flying creatures whom I can compare only to gigantic moths. With bright, luminous wings, upon the ebon forefront of the storm, they approached me in level but precipitate flight, and would have crashed headlong against the shut gate if they had not checked themselves with sudden, easy poise.

With hardly a flutter, they descended and paused on the ground beside me, supporting themselves on queer, delicate legs that branched at the knee-joints in floating antennae and waving tentacles. Their wings were sumptuously mottled webs of pearl and madder, opal and orange; their heads were circled by a series of convex and concave eyes, and fringed with coiling, hornlike organs from whose hollow ends there hung aerial filaments. I was startled and amazed by their aspect; but somehow, by an obscure telepathy I felt assured that their intentions toward me were friendly.

I knew that they wished to enter the city, and also that they understood my predicament. Nevertheless, I was not prepared for what happened. With movements of utmost celerity and grace, one of the giant, mothlike beings stationed himself at my right hand, and the other at my left. Then, before I could even suspect their intention, they enfolded my limbs and body with their long tentacles, wrapping me round and round as if with powerful ropes; and carrying me between them as if my weight were a mere trifle, they rose in the air and soared at the mighty ramparts!

In that swift and effortless ascent, the wall seemed to flow downward beside and beneath us, like a wave of molten stone. Dizzily, I watched the falling away of the mammoth blocks in endless recession. Then, we were level with the broad ramparts, were flying across the unguarded parapets and over a canyonlike space, toward the immense rectangular buildings and numberless square towers.

We had hardly crossed the walls when a weird, flickering glow was cast on the edifices before us by another lightening of the great cloud. The mothlike beings paid no apparent heed, and flew steadily on into the city with their strange faces toward an unseen goal. But, turning my head to peer backward at the storm, I beheld an astounding and appalling spectacle. Beyond the city ramparts, as if wrought by black magic or the toil of genii, another city had reared, and its high towers were moving swiftly forward beneath the rubescent dome of the burning cloud!

A second glance, and I perceived that the towers were identical with those I had beheld afar on the plain. In the interim of my passage through the woods, they had traveled over an expanse of many miles, by means of some unknown motive-power, and had closed in on the City of the Flame. Looking more closely, to determine the manner of their locomotion, I saw that they were not mounted on wheels, but on short, massy legs like jointed columns of metal, that gave them the stride of ungainly colossi. There were six or more of these legs to each tower, and near the tops of the towers were rows of huge eyelike openings, from which issued the bolts of red and violet flame I have mentioned before.

The many-colored forest had been burned away by these flames in a league-wide swath of devastation, even to the walls, and there was nothing but a stretch of black, vaporing desert between the mobile towers and the city. Then, even as I gazed, the long, leaping beams began to assail the craggy ramparts, and the topmost parapets were melting like lava beneath them. It was a scene of utmost terror and grandeur; but, a moment later, it was blotted from my vision by the buildings among which we had now plunged. The great lepidopterous creatures who bore me went on with the speed of eyrie-questing eagles. In the course of that flight, I was hardly capable of conscious thought or volition; I lived only in the breathless and giddy freedom of aerial movement, or dreamlike levitation above the labyrinthine maze of stone immensitudes and marvels. I was without actual cognisance of much that I beheld in that stupendous Babel of architectural imageries, and only afterward, in the more tranquil light of recollection, could I give coherent form and meaning to many of my impressions.

My senses were stunned by the vastness and strangeness of it all; I realized but dimly the cataclysmic ruin that was being loosed upon the city behind us, and the doom from which we were fleeing. I knew that war was being made with unearthly weapons and engineries, by inimical powers that I could not imagine, for a purpose beyond my conception; but, to me, it all had the elemental confusion and vague, impersonal horror of some cosmic catastrophe.

We flew deeper and deeper into the city. Broad, platform roofs and terracelike tiers of balconies flowed away beneath us, and the pavements raced like darkling streams at some enormous depth. Severe cubicular spires and square monoliths were all about and above us; and we saw on some of the roofs the dark, Atlantean people of the city, moving slowly and statuesquely, or standing in attitudes of cryptic resignation and despair, with their faces toward the flaming cloud. all were weaponless, and I saw no engineries anywhere such as might be used for purposes of military defense.

Swiftly as we flew, the climbing cloud was swifter, and the darkness of its intermittently glowing dome had over-arched the town while its spidery filaments had meshed the further heavens and would soon attach themselves to the opposite horizon. The buildings darkened and lightened with the recurrent fulguration, and I felt in all my tissues the painful pulsing of the thunderous vibrations.

Dully and vaguely, I realized that the winged beings who carried me between then were pilgrims to the Temple of the Flame. More and more, I became aware of an influence that must have been that of the starry music emanating from the temple's heart, There were soft, soothing vibrations in the air, that seemed to absorb and nullify the tearing discords of the unheard thunder. I felt that we were entering a zone of mystic refuge, or sidereal and celestial security, and my troubled senses were both lulled and exalted.

The gorgeous wings of the giant lepidopters began to slant downward. Before and beneath us, at some distance, I perceived a mammoth pile which I knew at once for the Temple of the Flame. Down, still down we went, in the awesome, space of the surrounding square; and then I was borne in through the lofty, ever-open entrance, and along the high hall with its thousand columns. Pregnant with strange balsams, the dim, mysterious dusk enfolded us, and we seemed to be entering realms of pre-mundane antiquity and trans-stellar immensity; to be following a pillared cavern that led to the core of some ultimate star.

It seemed that we were the last and only pilgrims, and also that the temple was deserted by its guardians, for we met no one in the whole extent of that column-crowded gloom. After a while, the dusk began to lighten, and we plunged into a widening beam of radiance, and then into the vast central chamber in which soared the fountain of green fire.

I remember only the impression of shadowy, flickering space, of a vault that was lost in the azure of infinity, of colossal and Memnonian statues that looked down from Himalayalike altitudes; and, above all, the dazzling jet of flame that aspired from a pit in the pavement and rose into the air like the visible rapture of gods. But all this I saw for an instant only. Then, I realized that the beings who bore me were flying straight toward the Flame on level wings, without the slightest pause or flutter of hesitation.

CHAPTER VI

THE INNER SPHERE

There was no room for fear, no time for alarm, in the dazed and chaotic turmoil of my sensations. I was stupefied by all that I had experienced, and moreover, the druglike spell of the Flame was upon me, even though I could not hear its fatal singing. I believe that I struggled a little, by some sort of mechanical muscular revulsion, against the tentacular arms that were wound about me. But the lepidopters gave no heed; it was plain that they were conscious of nothing but the mounting fire and its seductive music.

I remember, however, that there was no sensation of actual heat, such as might have been expected, when we neared the soaring column. Instead, I felt the most ineffable thrilling in all my fibers, as if I were being permeated by waves of celestial energy and demiurgic ecstasy. Then we entered the Flame …

Like Angarth before me, I had taken it for granted that the fate of all those who flung themselves into the Flame was an instant though blissful destruction. I expected to undergo a briefly flaring dissolution, followed by the nothingness of utter annihilation. The thing which really happened was beyond the boldest reach of speculative thought, and to give even a meager idea of my sensations would beggar the resources of language.

The Flame enfolded us like a green curtain, blotting from view the great chamber. Then it seemed to me that I was caught and carried to supercelestial heights, in an upward-rushing cataract of quintessential force and deific rapture, and an all-illuminating light. It seemed that I, and my companions, had achieved a godlike union with the Flame; that every atom of our bodies had undergone a transcendental expansion, and was winged with ethereal lightness.

It was as if we no longer existed, except as one divine, indivisible entity, soaring beyond the trammels of matter, beyond the limits of time and space, to attain undreamable shores. Unspeakable was the joy, and infinite the freedom of that ascent, in which we seemed to overpass the zenith of the highest star. Then, as if we had risen with the Flame to its culmination, had reached its very apex, we emerged and came to a pause.

My senses were faint with exaltation, my eyes blind with the glory of the fire; and the world on which I now gazed was a vast arabesque of unfamiliar forms and bewildering hues from another spectrum than the one to which our eyes are habituated. It swirled before my dizzy eyes like a labyrinth of gigantic jewels, with interweaving rays and tangled lustres, and only by slow degrees was I able to establish order and distinguish detail in the surging riot of my perceptions.

All about me were endless avenues of super-prismatic opal and jacinth; arches and pillars of ultraviolet gems, of transcendent sapphire, of unearthly ruby and amethyst, all suffused with a multi-tinted splendor. I appeared to be treading on jewels, and above me was a jeweled sky.

Presently, with recovered equilibrium, with eyes adjusted to a new range of cognition, I began to perceive the actual features of the landscape. With the two mothlike beings still beside me, I was standing on a million-flow-ered grass, among trees of a paradisal vegetation, with fruit, foliage, blossoms and trunks whose very forms were beyond the conception of tridimensional life. The grace of their drooping boughs, of their fretted fronds, was in-expressible in terms of earthly line and contour, and they seemed to be wrought of pure, ethereal substance, half translucent to the empyrean light, which accounted for the gemlike impression I had first received.

I breathed a nectar-laden air, and the ground beneath me was ineffably soft and resilient, as if it were com-posed of some higher form of matter than ours. My physical sensations were those of the utmost buoyancy and well-being, with no trace of fatigue or nervousness, such as might have been looked for after the unparalleled and marvellous events in which I had played a part. I felt no sense of mental dislocation or confusion; and, apart from my ability to recognize unknown colors and non-Euclidean forms, I began to experience a queer alteration and extension of tactility, through which it seemed that I was able to touch remote objects.

The radiant sky was filled with many-colored suns, like those that might shine on a world of some multiple solar system; but as I gazed, their glory became softer and dimmer, and the brilliant lustre of the trees and grass was gradually subdued, as if by encroaching twilight. I was beyond surprise, in the boundless marvel and mys-tery of it all, and nothing, perhaps, would have seemed incredible. But if anything could have amazed me or de-fied belief, it was the human face—the face of my van-ished friend, Giles Angarth, which now emerged. from among the waning jewels of the forest, followed by that of another man whom I recognized from photographs as Felix Ebbonly.

They came out from beneath the gorgeous boughs, and paused before me. Both were clad in lustrous fabrics, finer than Oriental silk, and of no earthly cut or pattern. Their look was both joyous and meditative, and their faces had taken on a hint of the same translucency that characterized the ethereal fruits and blossoms.

"We have been looking for you," said Angarth. "It occurred to me that, after reading my journal, you might be tempted to try the same experiment, if only to make sure whether the account was truth or fiction. This is Felix Ebbonly, whom I believe you have never met."

It surprised me when I found that I could hear his voice with perfect ease and clearness, and I wondered why the effect of the drug-soaked cotton should have died out so soon in my auditory nerves. Yet such details were trivial in the face of the astounding fact that I had found Angarth and Ebbonly; that they, as well as I, had survived the unearthly rapture of the Flame.

"Where are we?" I asked, after acknowledging his introduction. "I confess that I am totally at a loss to comprehend what has happened."

"We are now in what is called the Inner Dimension," explained Angarth. "It is a higher sphere of space and energy and matter than the one into which we were precipitated from Crater Ridge, and the only entrance is through the Singing Flame in the city of Ydmos. The Inner Dimension is born of the fiery fountain, and sustained by it; and those who fling themselves into the Flame are lifted thereby to this superior plane of vibration. For them, the Outer Worlds no longer exist. The nature of the Flame itself is not known, except that it is a fountain of pure energy springing from the central rock beneath Ydmos, and passing beyond mortal ken by virtue of its own ardency."

He paused, and seemed to be peering attentively at the winged entities, who still lingered at my side. Then, he continued:

"I haven't been here long enough to learn very much, myself; but I have found out a few things, and Ebbonly and I have established a sort of telepathic communication with the other beings who have passed through the Flame. Many of them have no spoken language, nor organs of speech, and their very methods of thought are basically different from ours, because of their divergent lines of sense-development and the varying conditions of the worlds from which they come. But we are able to communicate a few images.

"The persons who came with you are trying to tell me something," he went on. "You and they, it seems, are the last pilgrims who will enter Ydmos and attain the Inner Dimension. War is being made on the Flame and its guardians by the rulers of the Outer Lands, because so many of their people have obeyed the lure of the singing fountain and vanished into the higher sphere. Even now, their armies have closed in upon Ydmos and are blasting the city's ramparts with the force-bolts of their moving towers."

I told him what I had seen, comprehending, now, much that had been obscure heretofore. He listened gravely, and then said:

"It has long been feared that such war would be made sooner or later. There are many legends in the Outer Lands concerning the Flame and the fate of those who succumb to its attraction, but the truth is not known, or is guessed only by a few. Many believe, as I did, that the end is destruction; and by some who suspect its existence, the Inner Dimension is hated as a thing that lures idle dreamers away from worldly reality. It is regarded as a lethal and pernicious chimera, as a mere poetic dream, or a sort of opium paradise.

"There are a thousand things to tell you regarding the Inner Sphere, and the laws and conditions of being to which we are now subject after the revibration of all our component atoms in the Flame. But at present there is no time to speak further, since it is highly probable that we are all in grave danger—that the very existence of the Inner Dimension, as well as our own, is threatened by the inimical forces that are destroying Ydmos.

"There are some who say that the Flame is impregnable, that its pure essence will defy the blasting of all inferior beams, and its source remain impenetrable to the lightnings of the Outer Lords. But most are fearful of disaster, and expect the failure of the fountain itself when Ydmos is riven to the central rock.

"Because of this imminent peril, we must not tarry longer. There is a way which affords egress from the Inner Sphere to another and remoter Cosmos in a second infinity—a Cosmos unconceived by mundane astronomers, or by the astronomers of the worlds about Ydmos. The majority of the pilgrims, after a term of sojourn here, have gone on to the worlds of this other universe; and Ebbonly and I have waited only for your coming before following them. We must make haste, and delay no more, or doom will overtake us."

Even as he spoke, the two mothlike entities, seeming to resign me to the care of my human friends, arose on the jewel-tinted air and sailed in long, level flight above the paradisal perspectives whose remoter avenues were lost in glory. Angarth and Ebbonly had now stationed themselves beside me, and one took me by the left arm, and the other by the right.

"Try to imagine that you are flying," said Angarth. "In this sphere, levitation and flight are possible through willpower, and you will soon acquire the ability. We shall support and guide you, however, till you have grown accustomed to the new conditions and are independent of such help."

I obeyed his injunction, and formed a mental image of myself in the act of flying. I was amazed by the clearness and verisimilitude of the thought-picture, and still more by the fact that the picture was becoming an actuality! With little sense of effort, but with exactly the same feeling that characterizes a levitational dream, the three of us were soaring from the jeweled ground, slanting easily and swiftly upward through the glowing air.

Any attempt to describe the experience would be foredoomed to futility, since it seemed that a whole range of new senses had been opened up in me, together with corresponding thought-symbols for which there are no words in human speech. I was no longer Philip Hastane, but a larger, stronger and freer entity, differing as much from my former self as the personality developed beneath the influence of hashish or kava would differ. The dominant feeling was one of immense joy and liberation, coupled with a sense of imperative haste, of the need to escape into other realms where the joy would endure eternal and unthreatened.

My visual perceptions, as we flew above the burning, lucent woods, were marked by intense, aesthetic pleasure. It was as far above the normal delight afforded by agreeable imagery as the forms and colours of this world were beyond the cognition of normal eyes. Every changing image was a source of veritable ecstasy; and the ecstasy mounted as the whole landscape began to brighten again and returned to the flashing, scintillating glory it had worn when I first beheld it.

CHAPTER VII

THE DESTRUCTION OF YDMOS

We soared at a lofty elevation, looking down on numberless miles of labyrinthine forest, on long, luxurious meadows, on voluptuously folded hills, on palatial buildings, and waters that were clear as the pristine lakes and rivers of Eden. It all seemed to quiver and pulsate like one living effulgent, ethereal entity, and waves of radiant rapture passed from sun to sun in the splendor-crowded heaven.

As we went on, I noticed again, after an interval, that partial dimming of the light; that somnolent, dreamy saddening of the colors, to be followed by another period of ecstatic brightening. The slow tidal rhythm of this process appeared to correspond to the rising and falling of the Flame, as Angarth had described it in his journal, and I suspected immediately that there was some connection. No sooner had I formulated this thought, than I became aware that Angarth was speaking. And yet, I am not sure whether he spoke, or whether his worded thought was perceptible to me through another sense than that of physical audition. At any rate, I was cognisant of his comment:

"You are right. The waning and waxing of the fountain and its music is perceived in the Inner Dimension as a clouding and lightening of all visual images."

Our flight began to swiften, and I realized that my companions were employing all their psychic energies in an effort to redouble our speed. The lands below us blurred to a cataract of streaming color, a sea of flowing luminosity; and we seemed to be hurtling onward like stars through the fiery air. The ecstasy of that endless soaring, the anxiety of that precipitate flight from an unknown doom, are incommunicable. But I shall never forget them, nor the state of ineffable communion and understanding that existed between the three of us. The memory of it all is housed in the deepest, most abiding cells of my brain.

Others were flying beside and above and beneath us, now, in the fluctuant glory: pilgrims of hidden worlds and occult dimensions, proceeding as we ourselves toward that other Cosmos of which the Inner Sphere was the antechamber. These beings were strange and outré beyond belief, in their corporeal forms and attributes; and yet I took no thought of their strangeness, but felt toward them the same conviction of fraternity that I felt toward Angarth and Ebbonly.

As we still went on, it appeared to me that my two companions were telling me many things; communicating, by what means I am not sure, much that they had learned in their new existence. With a grave urgency as if, perhaps, the time for imparting this information night well be brief, ideas were expressed and conveyed which I could never have understood amid terrestrial circumstances. Things that were inconceivable in terms of the five senses, or in abstract symbols of philosophic or mathematic thought, were made plain to me as the letters of the alphabet.

Certain of these data, however, are roughly conveyable or suggestible in language. I was told of the gradual process of initiation into the life of the new dimension, of the powers gained by the neophyte during his term of adaptation, of the various recondite, aesthetic joys experienced through a mingling and multiplying of all the perceptions, of the control acquired over natural forces and over matter itself, so that raiment could be woven and buildings reared solely through an act of volition.

I learned, also, of the laws that would control our passage to the further Cosmos, and the fact that such passage was difficult and dangerous for anyone who had not lived a certain length of time in the Inner Dimension. Likewise, I was told that no one could return to our present plane from the higher Cosmos, even as no one could go backward through the Flame into Ydmos.

Angarth and Ebbonly had dwelt long enough in the Inner Dimension, they said, to be eligible for entrance to the worlds beyond; and they thought that I, too, could escape through their assistance, even though I had not yet developed the faculty of spatial equilibrium necessary to sustain those who dared the interspheric path and its dreadful subjacent gulfs alone. There were boundless, unforeseeable realms, planet on planet, universe on universe, to which we might attain, and among whose prodigies and marvels we could dwell or wander indefinitely. In these worlds, our brains would be attuned to the comprehension of vaster and higher scientific laws, and states of entity beyond those of our present dimensional milieu.

I have no idea of the duration of our flight; since, like everything else, my sense of time was completely altered and transfigured. Relatively speaking, we may have gone on for hours; but it seemed to me that we had crossed an area of that supernal terrain for whose transit many years, or even centuries, might well have been required.

Even before we came within sight of it, a clear pictorial image of our destination had arisen in my mind, doubtless through some sort of thought-transference. I seemed to envision a stupendous mountain range, with alp on celestial alp, higher than the summer cumuli on Earth; and above them all the horn of an ultraviolet peak whose head was enfolded in a hueless and spiral cloud, touched with the sense of invisible chromatic overtones, that seemed to come down upon it from skies beyond the zenith. I knew that the way to the Outer Cosmos was hidden in the high cloud....

On and on we soared; and at length the mountain range appeared on the far horizon, and I saw the paramount peak of ultraviolet with its dazzling crown of cumulus. Nearer still we came, till the strange volutes of cloud were almost above us, towering to the heavens and vanishing among the varicolored suns; and we saw the gleaming forms of pilgrims who preceded us, as they entered the swirling folds. At this moment, the sky and the landscape had flamed again to their culminating brilliance; they burned with a thousand hues and lusters, so that the sudden, unlooked-for eclipse which now occurred was all the more complete and terrible. Before I was conscious of anything amiss, I seemed to hear a despairing cry from my friends, who must have felt the oncoming calamity through a subtler sense than any of which I was yet capable. Then, beyond the high and luminescent alp of our destination, I saw the mounting of a wall of darkness, dreadful and instant, positive and palpable, that rose everywhere and toppled like some Atlantean wave upon the irised suns and the fiery-colored vistas of the Inner Dimension.

We hung irresolute in the shadowed air, powerless and hopeless before the impending catastrophe, and saw that the darkness had surrounded the entire world and was rushing upon us from all sides. It ate the heavens, blotted the outer suns, and the vast perspectives over which we had flown appeared to shrink and shrivel like a fire-blackened paper. We seemed to wait alone, for one terrible instant, in a center of dwindling light on which the cyclonic forces of night and destruction were impinging with torrential rapidity.

The center shrank to a mere point—and then the darkness was upon us like an overwhelming maelstrom, like the falling and crashing of Cyclopean walls. I seemed to go down with the wreck of shattered worlds in a roaring sea of vortical space and force, to descend into some infra-stellar pit, some ultimate limbo to which the shards of forgotten suns and systems are flung. Then, after a measureless interval, there came the sensation of violent impact, as if I had fallen among these shards, at the bottom of the universal night.

I struggled back to consciousness with slow, prodigious effort, as if I were crushed beneath some irremovable weight, beneath the lightless and inert débris of galaxies. It seemed to require the labors of a Titan to lift my lids, and my body and limbs were heavy, as if they had been turned to some denser element than human flesh, or had been subjected to the gravitation of a grosser planet than the Earth.

My mental processes were benumbed and painful, and confused to the last degree; but at length I realized that I was lying on a riven and tilted pavement, among gigantic blocks of fallen stone. Above me, the light of a livid heaven came down among overturned and jagged walls that no longer supported their colossal dome. Close beside me, I saw a fuming pit from which a ragged rift extended through the floor, like the chasm wrought by an earthquake.

I could not recognize my surroundings for a time; but at last, with a toilsome groping of thought, I understood that I was lying in the ruined temple of Ydmos, and that the pit whose gray and acrid vapours rose beside me was that from which the fountain of singing flame had issued. It was a scene of stupendous havoc and devastation: the wrath that had been visited upon Ydmos had left no wall nor pylon of the temple standing. I stared at the blighted heavens from an architectural ruin in which the remains of On and Angkor would have been mere rubble-heaps.

With Herculean effort, I turned my head away from the smoking pit, whose thin, sluggish fumes curled upward in phantasmal coils where the green ardour of the Flame had soared and sung. Not until then did I perceive my companions. Angarth, still insensible, was lying near at hand, and just beyond him I saw the pale, contorted face of Ebbonly, whose lower limbs and body were pinned down by the rough and broken pediment of a fallen pillar.

Striving, as in some eternal nightmare, to throw off the leaden-clinging weight of my inertia, and able to bestir myself only with the most painful slowness and laboriousness, I got to my feet and went over to Ebbonly. Angarth, I saw at a glance, was uninjured and would presently regain consciousness, but Ebbonly, crushed by the monolithic mass of stone, was dying swiftly, and even with the help of a dozen men I could not have released him from his imprisonment; nor could I have done anything to palliate his agony.

He tried to smile, with gallant and piteous courage, as I stooped above him.

"It's no use—I'm going in a moment," he whispered. "Good-bye, Hastane—and tell Angarth good-bye for me, too."

His tortured lips relaxed, his eyelids dropped and his head fell back on the temple pavement. With an unreal dreamlike horror, almost without emotion, I saw that he was dead. The exhaustion that still beset me was too profound to permit of thought or feeling; it was like the first reaction that follows the awakening from a drug-debauch. My nerves were like burnt-out wires, my muscles dead and unresponsive as clay; my brain was ashen and gutted, as if a great fire had burned within it and gone out.

Somehow, after an interval of whose length my memory is uncertain, I managed to revive Angarth, and he sat up dully and dazedly. When I told him that Ebbonly was dead, my words appeared to make no impression upon him, and I wondered for a while if he understood. Finally, rousing himself a little with evident difficulty, he peered at the body of our friend, and seemed to realize in some measure the horror of the situation. But I think he would have remained there for hours, or perhaps for all time, in his utter despair and lassitude, if I had not taken the initiative.

"Come," I said, with an attempt at firmness. "We must get out of this."

"Where to?" he queried, dully. "The Flame has failed at its source, and the Inner Dimension is no more. I wish I were dead, like Ebbonly—I might as well be, judging from the way I feel."

"We must find our way back to Crater Ridge," I said. "Surely we can do it, if the inter-dimensional portals have not been destroyed."

Angarth did not seem to hear me, but he followed obediently when I took him by the arm and began to seek an exit from the temple's heart, among the roofless halls and overturned columns....

My recollections of our return are dim and confused, and full of the tediousness of some interminable delirium. I remember looking back at Ebbonly, lying white and still beneath the massive pillar that would serve as his eternal monument; and I recall the mountainous ruins of the city, in which it seemed that we were the only living beings. It was a wilderness of chaotic stone, of fused, obsidianlike blocks, where streams of molten lava still ran in the mighty chasms, or poured like torrents adown unfathomable pits that had opened in the ground. And I remember seeing, amid the wreckage, the charred bodies of those dark colossi who were the people of Ydmos and the warders of the Flame.

Like pygmies lost in some shattered fortalice of the giants, we stumbled onward, strangling in mephitic and metallic vapors, reeling with weariness, dizzy with the heat that emanated everywhere to surge upon us in buffeting waves. The way was blocked by overthrown buildings, by toppled towers and battlements, over which we climbed precariously and toilsomely; and often we were compelled to divagate from our direct course by enormous rifts that seemed to cleave the foundations of the world.

The moving towers of the wrathful Outer Lords had withdrawn; their armies had disappeared on the plain beyond Ydmos, when we staggered over the riven, shapeless and scoriac crags that had formed the city's ramparts. Before us was nothing but desolation—a fire-blackened and vapor-vaulted expanse in which no tree or blade of grass remained.

Across this waste we found our way to the slope of violet grass above the plain, which had lain beyond the path of the invader's bolts. There the guiding monoliths, reared by a people of whom we were never to learn even the name, still looked down upon the fuming desert and the mounded wrack of Ydmos. And there, at length, we came once more to the grayish-green columns that were the gateway between the worlds.

www.ingramcontent.com/pod-product-compliance
Lightning Source LLC
Chambersburg PA
CBHW050906120626
46554CB00003B/1043